MOG
the Forgetful Cat

MOG
the Forgetful Cat

written and
illustrated by
Judith Kerr

HarperCollins *Children's Books*

For our own Mog

Other books by Judith Kerr include:

Mog's Christmas*	Mog's Bad Thing*
Mog and the Baby*	Goodbye Mog
Mog in the Dark	Birdie Halleluyah!
Mog's Amazing Birthday Caper*	The Tiger Who Came to Tea*
Mog and Bunny	The Other Goose
Mog and Barnaby	Goose in a Hole
Mog on Fox Night	Twinkles, Arthur and Puss*
Mog and the Granny	One Night in the Zoo
Mog and the V.E.T.*	*also available on audio CD.

First published in hardback in Great Britain by William Collins Sons & Co Ltd in 1970. First published in paperback in 1975
and in a new edition in 1993 by Picture Lions. Reissued by HarperCollins Children's Books in 2005. This edition published in 2010.

10 9 8 7 6 5 4 3 2

ISBN-13: 978-0-00-723721-0

Visit our website at: www.harpercollins.co.uk

Printed in China

Mr Thomas

Mrs Thomas

Nicky

Debbie

Once there was a cat called Mog.
She lived with a family called Thomas.
Mog was nice but not very clever.
She didn't understand a lot of things.
A lot of other things she forgot.
She was a very forgetful cat.

Sometimes she ate her supper.
Then she forgot that she had
eaten it.

Sometimes she thought of something
in the middle of washing her leg.
Then she forgot to wash the rest of it.

Once she forgot
that cats can't fly.

But most of all she forgot her cat flap.
The cat flap led from the kitchen
into the garden.
Mog could go out…

…and in
again.
It was
her
own
little
door.

The garden always made Mog very excited.
She smelled all the smells.
She chased the birds.
She climbed the trees.
She ran round and round
with a big fluffed-up tail.
And then she forgot the cat flap.
She forgot that she had a cat flap.
She wanted to go back into the house,
but she couldn't remember how.

In the end she sat outside the kitchen window
and meowed until someone let her in.

Afterwards you could always tell
where she had sat.
This made Mr Thomas very sad.
He said, "Bother that cat!"
But Debbie said, "She's nice!"

Once Mog had a very bad day.
Even the start of the day was bad.
Mog was still asleep.
Then Nicky picked her up.
He hugged her
and said, "Nice kitty!"
Mog said nothing.
But she was not happy.

Then it was breakfast time.
Mog forgot that cats have milk for breakfast.
She forgot that cats only have eggs as a treat.

She ate an egg for her breakfast.
Mrs Thomas said, "Bother that cat!"
Debbie said, "Nicky doesn't like eggs anyway."

Mog looked through her cat flap.
It was raining in the garden.
Mog thought, "Perhaps the sun is shining in the street."
When the milkman came she ran out.
The milkman shut the door.

The sun was not shining in the street after all.
It was raining.
A big dog came down the street.
Mog ran.
The dog ran too.

Mog ran right round the house.
And the dog ran after her.
She climbed over the fence.
She ran through the garden
and jumped up outside the kitchen window.
She meowed a big meow,
very sudden and very loud.

Mrs Thomas said, "Bother that cat!"
Debbie said, "It wasn't her fault."

Mog was very sleepy.
She found a nice warm, soft place
and went to sleep.
She had a lovely dream.
Mog dreamed that she had wings.

She could fly everywhere.
She could fly faster than the birds,
even quite big birds…
Suddenly she woke up.

Mrs Thomas said, "Bother that cat!"
Debbie said, "I think you look nicer without a hat."

Debbie gave Mog her supper
and Mog ate it all up.
Then Debbie and Nicky went to bed.

Mog had a rest too,
but Mr Thomas wanted to see the fight.
Mr Thomas said, "Bother that cat!"

Mog thought, "Nobody likes me."
Then she thought, "Debbie likes me."
Debbie's door was open.

Debbie's bed was warm.
Debbie's hair was soft, like kitten fur.
Mog forgot that Debbie was not a kitten.

Debbie had a dream.
It was a bad dream.
It was a dream about a tiger.

The tiger wanted
to eat Debbie.
It was licking her hair.

Debbie shouted.
Mog jumped.
Mr and Mrs Thomas said,
"Bother, bother,
BOTHER that cat!"
Debbie said nothing.
She was still crying
because of the bad dream.

Mog ran out of the room
and right through the house
and out of her cat flap.
She was very sad.
The garden was dark.
The house was dark too.
Mog sat in the dark
and thought dark thoughts.
She thought, "Nobody likes me.
They've all gone to bed.
There's no one to let me in.
And they haven't even given me my supper."

Then she noticed something.
The house was not quite dark.
There was a little light moving about.
She looked through the window
and saw a man in the kitchen.
Mog thought, "Perhaps that man will let me in.
Perhaps he will give me my supper."

She meowed her biggest meow,
very sudden and very, very loud.
The man was surprised.
He dropped his bag.
It made a big noise
and everyone in the house woke up.

Mr Thomas ran down to the kitchen
and shouted, "A burglar!"
The burglar said, "Bother that cat!"
Mrs Thomas telephoned the police.
Debbie let Mog in
and Nicky hugged her.

A policeman came and they told him what had happened.
The policeman looked at Mog.
He said, "What a remarkable cat.

I've seen watch-dogs, but never a watch-cat.
She will get a medal."
Debbie said, "I think she'd rather have an egg."

Mog had a medal.

She also had an egg every day for breakfast.

Mr and Mrs Thomas told all their friends about her.

They said, "Mog is really remarkable."

And they never – (or almost never) – said, "Bother that cat!"